Francis Nona

The fall of the Alamo

An historical drama in four acts concluded by an epilogue entitled The

battle of San Jacinto

Francis Nona

The fall of the Alamo
An historical drama in four acts concluded by an epilogue entitled The battle of San Jacinto

ISBN/EAN: 9783337303815

Printed in Europe, USA, Canada, Australia, Japan

Cover: Foto ©Andreas Hilbeck / pixelio.de

More available books at **www.hansebooks.com**

Charter,
By-Laws and
House Rules
Of...

The Dallas Club

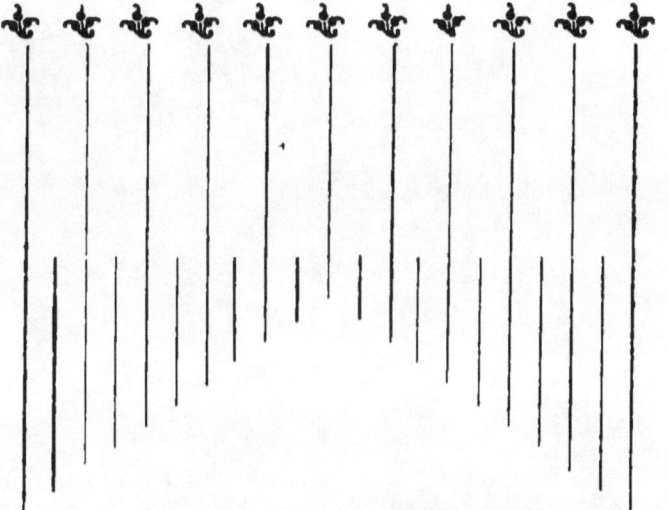

Chartered
March 12, 1887
Organized
March 21, 1887

Officers

Officers, 1899-1900

W. L. HALL, ... President
CHAS. FRED TUCKER, ... Vice-President
BENNETT HILL, ... Secretary
J. B. ADOUE, ... Treasurer

Directors

L. SHERWOOD SABIN. PAUL A. FLORIAN.

M. B. SHANNON. M. L. KAUFMAN.

J. B. ADOUE. BENNETT HILL.

HUNTER A. CRAYCROFT. W. L. HALL.

CHAS. FRED TUCKER.

House Committee

H. A. CRAYCROFT, Chairman.

J. M. CARY. M. B. SHANNON.

Library Committee

M. L. KAUFMAN, Chairman.

E. DICK SLAUGHTER. H. L. SEAY.

Membership Committee

PAUL A. FLORIAN, Chairman.

J. T. MURPHY. T. L. CAMP.

Charter

Charter

ARTICLE I. The name of this Corporation shall be "THE DALLAS CLUB."

ART. II. The purposes and objects of this Corporation are the encouragement of social intercourse among its members, the support of literary undertakings, the encouragement of the study and cultivation of literature, the maintenance of a library and reading room, and the promotion of the fine arts.

ART. III. The place of business of this Corporation shall be in the City of Dallas, in Dallas County, Texas.

ART. IV. This Corporation shall have existence and continue for a term of fifty years from the date of the filing of this Charter in the office of the Secretary of State.

ART. V. The number of the Directors of this Corporation shall be nine. The Directors for the first year of the existence of this Corporation shall be George W. Toland, B. A. Pope, R. V. Tompkins, J. C. O'Connor, A. Sanger, Thos. T. Holloway, F. M. Cockrell, John N. Simpson and Alfred Davis, all of whom are residents of the City of Dallas, Texas.

ART. VI. The amount of the Capital Stock of this Corporation is authorized to be fifty thousand dollars, to be divided into five hundred shares of one hundred dollars each. This Corporation is authorized to begin business as soon as twenty thousand dollars of the Capital Stock shall have been subscribed. No one, unless he be a member of this, THE DALLAS CLUB, shall own or subscribe to stock. Membership shall be constituted in such manner as the By-Laws may direct. No one individual shall own, hold or subscribe to more than twenty-five shares of stock. No one shall become or shall be a member of THE DALLAS CLUB unless he hold at least one share of stock.

ART. VII. This Corporation is authorized to acquire, purchase and hold such real, personal and mixed property as may be necesaary for the convenient accomplishment of the purposes hereinbefore specified.

(Signed)

GEO. W. TOLAND.
R. V. TOMPKINS.
B. A. POPE.
J. C. O'CONNOR.
F. M. COCKRELL.
THOS. T. HOLLOWAY.

STATE OF TEXAS,
 COUNTY OF DALLAS. }

Before me, the undersigned authority, on this day personally appeared Geo. W. Toland, R. V. Tompkins, B. A. Pope, J. C. O'Connor, F. M. Cockrell and Thos. T. Holloway, known to me to be the persons who executed and signed the foregoing instrument, and acknowledged to me that they executed the same for the purposes and considerations therein expressed.

In Witness Whereof, I have hereunto set my hand and official seal, this 9th day of March, A. D. 1887.

(Signed)   LAFAYETTE FITZHUGH,
(Seal)   Notary Public Dallas Co.

(ENDORSED)

Charter: The Dallas Club, filed in the Department of State, March 12, 1887.

(Signed)   J. M. MOORE,
                Secretary of State.

THE STATE OF TEXAS, }
  DEPARTMENT OF STATE. }

I, J. M. Moore, Secretary of the State of Texas, do hereby certify that the foregoing is a true copy of the original Charter of "THE DALLAS CLUB," with the endorsements thereon, now on file in this Department.

        Witness my official signature and the seal of
        State affixed, at the City of Austin, this
(Seal)   12th day of March, 1887.
    (Signed)   J. M. MOORE,
                       Secretary of State.

                DALLAS CLUB, }
             January 12, 1899. }

At a meeting of the Board of Directors of The Dallas Club, on the date above mentioned, W. L. Hall, President, and Bennett Hill, Secretary, the following Directors being present, viz: W. L. Hall, T. L. Camp, Wm. Thompson, J. B. Adoue and Bennett Hill, the following By-Laws and House Rules were adopted, to take effect from and after the 12th day of January, 1899:

By-Laws

By-Laws

RULE I.

STOCK AND STOCKHOLDERS.

SECTION 1. Only members of the Club shall be stockholders. No stockholder shall be entitled to vote unless he shall have paid the amount of his stock or who shall be in arrear in his dues to the Club.

SEC. 2. Any stockholder upon ceasing to be a member of the Club by resignation, expulsion or otherwise, shall within six months thereafter dispose of his stock to a member, and upon his failure to do so his stock may be sold to the highest bidder for cash at the Club, after giving notice to the holder of said stock for ten days and advertising same by posting notices of such sale in the Club rooms for twenty days prior thereto, the proceeds to be paid over to such stockholder; and the share of any stockholder who is indebted to the Club and has been in default for thirty days, and refuses to pay on demand, may be disposed of in the same way in satisfaction of the amount due the Club, any balance to be paid over to him.

SEC. 3. Stock shall be transferred only on the books of the corporation and no stock shall be transferred if any indebtedness is due the Club by the transferrer, or until such indebtedness is paid in full.

SEC. 4. Certificates of stock shall be signed by the President and attested by the Secretary, and under the seal of the corporation.

Sec. 5. All dues or other indebtedness owing by any stockholder to the Club shall be a charge upon his stock.

RULE II.

MEETINGS OF STOCKHOLDERS.

Section 1. There shall be an annual meeting of the stockholders on the third Monday in January of each year. Notice of the time and place of such meeting, signed by the Secretary of the Club, shall be published, at least ten days previous to such meeting, in some daily paper published in the city of Dallas.

Sec. 2. Special meetings of stockholders may be called by the Directory; special meetings shall also be called by the President upon the written request of thirty (30) or more stockholders filed with the Secretary. Calls for special meetings of stockholders shall set forth the objects of the meeting and no other business shall be transacted than that named in the call. At least five (5) days' notice of special meetings shall be given in such manner as the President may direct.

Sec. 3. Thirty (30) members shall constitute a quorum at the annual meeting of stockholders. Twenty (20) members shall constitute a quorum at a special meeting.

Sec. 4. No stockholder shall vote by proxy.

Sec. 5. At all meetings of stockholders each stockholder shall be entitled to one vote only, irrespective of the number of shares he may hold in the corporation.

RULE III.

DIRECTORS.

Section 1. The management of the corporation shall be under the control of the Directory.

Sec. 2. Nine (9) Directors shall be elected at the annual meeting of the stockholders in each year. The Directors shall serve for one year and until their successors shall be elected and qualified. Acceptance of the office of Director shall be all the qualification necessary.

Sec. 3. The Directors shall elect of their number a President and vice-President, and shall appoint a Secretary and Treasurer, each to serve for one year, and until his successor shall be appointed and qualified. And the Directors shall also appoint an assistant to the Secretary, who shall not necessarily be a Director or stockholder.

Sec. 4. The Directory shall hold a regular meeting on the second Saturday in each month and they shall also hold special meetings when called together by the President or vice-President; and upon the request of any three members of the Directory, the President or vice-President shall call such special meeting.

Sec. 5. Vacancies in the Directory or in the offices of the Club shall be filled by the Directory.

Sec. 6. In case of failure from any cause to elect Directors at the annual meeting of stockholders, the President shall call a special meeting of stockholders to elect Directors.

SEC. 7. The Directory shall adopt regulations known as House Rules, for the government of the Club.

SEC. 8. Club dues, in such amount as the necessities of the Club may require, shall be established by the Directory.

RULE IV.

THE PRESIDENT.

The President shall preside at all meetings of the Directory and of the stockholders. He shall not vote except in case of a tie.

RULE V.

THE VICE-PRESIDENT.

In the absence of the President the powers and duties of the President shall devolve upon the vice-President.

RULE VI.

THE SECRETARY AND TREASURER.

SECTION 1. The Assistant Secretary shall keep full and accurate minutes of the proceedings of all meetings of the corporation and of the Directors or House Committee; shall notify the Directors of all meetings of the Board, and shall perform such other duties as the Directory may require. He shall collect all moneys due the Club and shall receive such moneys as the Directory may order, and shall pay them over to the Treasurer, taking his receipts therefor. He shall keep the accounts, books and papers of the corporation except those in charge of the Treasurer, and shall deliver the same at the end of the term of his employment to the Secretary. The Secretary shall be the custodian of the corporate seal, shall attest certificates of stock, and shall have general supervision and control of the Assistant Secretary in the discharge of his duties in keeping the books, accounts and minutes of the Club. It shall be the duty of the Secretary to report to the Directors from time to time as to the manner in which said duties are being discharged. The Secretary shall not be authorized to receive or collect any money, nor shall he be in any way responsible for the same, and no bond shall be required of him. The Secretary shall receive no compensation for his services. The Assistant Secretary shall be paid for the performance of his duty such a sum of money as may be fixed by the Directors, and his term of employment shall be at the will of the Directory and for such a term as may be fixed by contract with him.

SEC. 2. Before entering upon the duties of his office, the Assistant Secretary shall give bond in the sum of $3,000.00, to be approved by the Directory, conditioned that he shall faithfully perform all his duties as Assistant Secretary and pay over and account for all moneys of the Club received by him.

SEC. 3. The Treasurer shall receive and receipt for all moneys of the corporation, shall have custody of the same by direction of the Directory, keeping a record thereof, and proper vouchers for all disbursements. He shall make report annually, and as often as required by the Board of Directors, of all receipts and disbursements, and shall, upon the appointment and qualification of his successor, deliver to him all moneys, books and papers pertaining to his office.

SEC. 4. All checks and orders for money shall be signed "Dallas Club, per..Assistant Secretary," and countersigned by the President, or, in his absence, by the Secretary or vice-President, and the Treasurer shall disburse no funds of the Club except upon such written order.

The President, or, in his absence, the vice-President and Secretary, shall sign no order for funds of the Club except by order of the Directory or upon bill approved by at least two members of the House Committee.

SEC. 5. Before entering upon the duties of his office the Treasurer shall give bond in the sum of three thousand dollars ($3,000.00), with two or more sureties, to be approved by the Directors, conditioned that he shall faithfully perform all the duties of the office.

RULE VII.

MEMBERSHIP.

SECTION 1. The members of the Club shall be classed, for Club purposes, as resident members, non-resident members and honorary members. Resident members shall be those residing in the county of Dallas. All members not residing in the county of Dallas shall be non-resident members. No one shall be elected an honorary member save by the unanimous vote of the Directory. Honorary members shall not pay Club dues.

SEC. 2. The number of resident members shall not exceed three hundred (300).

RULE VIII.

APPOINTMENT OF COMMITTEES.

The Directors may appoint such standing or special committees as they shall see fit. They shall appoint a committee of three members who, with the President and Secretary, shall constitute a committee on membership. They shall also appoint a House Committee of three members.

RULE IX.

ELECTION TO MEMBERSHIP.

SECTION 1. No one shall be elected to membership in the Club except upon a unanimous vote of the Committee on Membership.

SEC. 2. Every candidate for admission must be proposed by one member and seconded by another, other than the members of the Committee on Membership. The names, residences and occupation of gentlemen proposed for membership shall be inserted in a book provided for the purpose, the names of such proposer and seconder being in their respective handwriting, and the name of such candidate, with the names of his proposer and seconder, shall be posted in the Club rooms for at least ten (10) days prior to action thereon by the Committee on Membership.

The names of gentlemen failing to be elected shall not be proposed again for six months.

SEC. 3. The Secretary shall report upon the result of the election to each applicant, simply stating that his application has been accepted or rejected.

SEC. 4. Objections to the admission of a candidate may be made to any member of the Committee on Membership before action thereon by the committee. In case three resident members object to the admission of any applicant his name shall be withdrawn. The names of members objecting shall not be divulged outside the Membership Committee.

SEC. 5. Every person elected shall, within ten days after being informed thereof by the Assistant Secretary, pay to said Assistant Secretary his entrance or initiation fee and first monthly dues and shall then, and not otherwise, be a member of the Club, and in case he shall fail so to do his election shall be void.

SEC. 6. To become a resident member the applicant shall pay an entrace fee of twenty-five ($25.00) dollars besides being the owner of at least one fully paid up share of stock in the corporation.

SEC. 7. Non-residents of Dallas county may be admitted upon payment in advance of an initiation fee of twenty-five dollars ($25.00), provided, that they be proposed and elected in accordance with the foregoing section of this rule. Such members shall be entitled to all the privileges accorded to regular members, except that of voting or holding office, but they shall not be required to own stock.

SEC. 8. Members not indebted to the Club, who remove permanently from Dallas county, may be placed upon the list of non-resident members by notifying the Secretary in writing of their change of residence.

Sec. 9. The annual dues of resident members shall be thirty-six dollars ($36.00) payable in monthly installments of three dollars ($3.00) each *on the first day of each month in advance*. The annual dues of non-resident members shall be ten dollars ($10.00), *payable annually in advance*.

RULE X.

RESIGNATION.

No resignation shall be accepted by the Directory if the member be in arrear in his dues to the Club.

RULE XI.

The Directory may expel or may drop from the roll of membership any member for non-payment of dues, or indebtedness to the Club, for conduct unbecoming a gentleman, or for conduct calculated to endanger the welfare of the Club, or for violation of any By-Laws or House Rules. But before any member shall be expelled or dropped from the rolls a notice shall be mailed to him, at his address as it appears on the Club books, at least ten (10) days before his case is acted upon by the Directory, requesting him to show cause why he should not be expelled or dropped from the rolls.

RULE XII.

The name of every member failing to pay his dues *within one month after the same become due* shall be placed in a frame provided for such notices, of which the Assistant Secretary shall inform him in writing and if said dues are not paid within thirty (30) days thereafter, he shall cease to be a member of the Club and his name shall be erased from the books, unless he can show satisfactory reasons for the non-payment thereof to the Board of Directors. *Provided, however,* that before any member shall be dropped from the rolls, a notice shall be mailed to him at his address, as it appears on the Club books, at least ten days before his case is acted upon, requesting him to show cause why he should not be dropped from the rolls.

RULE XIII.

All indebtedness to the Club on account of bar, restaurant and sleeping rooms shall be due on the first day of the month succeeding the one in which it was contracted; and if not paid by the tenth day of said month, then the Assistant Secretary shall proceed to post the delinquents and they shall be subject to be dropped from the rolls as provided for in Rule XII.

RULE XIV.

If any member shall cease to be a stockholder in the corporation by transfer of his stock, forfeiture or otherwise, his membership shall be entirely terminated.

RULE XV.

THE HOUSE COMMITTEE.

The House Committee shall meet at least once in each week. They shall make all current purchases for the ordinary uses of the Club or direct the same to be made; regulate the prices to be charged for all articles used in the Club; appoint and dismiss all employes and fix their compensation and otherwise superintend and direct the ordinary and current affairs of the Club. But they shall not make any unusual or extraordinary purchases, or permanent improvements, or alterations in the Club property, or give any entertainments, or incur any extraordinary expenses of any kind without first consulting and being advised by the Directory.

RULE XVI.

AMENDMENTS.

The Directors may adopt By-Laws for the government of the corporation and may amend or repeal the same, but such By-Laws may be altered, changed or amended by a majority vote of the stockholders, at any election or special meeting ordered for that purpose by the Directors on a written application of a majority of the stockholders.

House Rules

House Rules

It is the duty of every member of the Club to make himself familiar with its laws and rules, and ignorance thereof shall never be admissible in excuse for any breach or neglect of the same.

Rule 1.

The Club rooms shall be opened at 8 o'clock, A. M. from November 1st to May 1st, and at 7 o'clock, A. M. from May 1st to November 1st. Members will not be admitted after 1 o'clock, A. M. The house will be closed at 2 o'clock, A. M., and lights turned off.

Rule 2.

The wine room will be closed at 1 o'clock, A. M. No refreshments, excepting drinks, shall be served in the library or sitting room.

Rule 3.

Credit extended to the members in the wine room or restaurant shall be in the discretion of the House Committee, which committee may at any time refuse credit to any member. Any member introducing a visitor will be responsible for any debts contracted by him.

Rule 4.

Payments should be made to Assistant Secretary at office in Club building.

Rule 5.

No newspapers, magazines, books or other articles, the property of the Club, shall be removed from the Club floor by any member or employe.

Rule 6.

Newspapers, magazines and books of the Club shall not be marked or otherwise defaced.

Rule 7.

No member or visitor shall be allowed to give, under any pretense whatever, money or any gratuity to any one in the service of the Club.

Rule 8.

No member or visitor shall be allowed to send a servant of the Club out of the building, unless by the permission of the President, Secretary, Assistant Secretary or a member of the House Committee.

Rule 9.

Subscription papers shall not be circulated or exposed in the Club rooms pertaining to anything foreign to the Club. Dogs shall not be allowed in the building.

Rule 10.

All requests and complaints must be made in writing, signed and addressed to the House Committee or to the Directory, and deposited in the locked box provided for the purpose.

Rule 11.

No complaints addressed personally to the members of the House Committee or to the Directory or to any officer of the Club, will receive attention unless presented in accordance with Rule 10.

Rule 12.

Strangers, not residing in Dallas or its suburbs, can be introduced as visitors for a period of one week, upon registering their names and obtaining a card for them signed by the Assistant Secretary. This time may be extended at the discretion of the President or the House Committee.

Persons not members of the Club, residing or engaged in business in Dallas or its suburbs, shall not, under *any pretext whatever, be admitted as visitors to the Club*.

Rule 13.

ASSISTANT SECRETARY.

The Assistant Secretary shall be subject to the control of the House Committee. He shall reside in the Club House, and will have the custody of the plate, china, glass, etc. He will have the general control and superintendence of the servants and be responsible for their conduct and cleanly appearance. He is required to notify members of any violation of the regulations and to report the same to the House Committee. The servants' entrance in the rear will be under lock, and servants must not enter or go out of the Club, except by the servants' entrance at the rear of the building. Articles of glass, earthenware, etc., which may be broken by the members, either in the dining room or elsewhere in the building, shall be paid for by them.

Rule 14.

The House Committee shall appoint a janitor and janitress. The duty of the janitor and janitress shall be as follows: Superintendence of heating, opening and closing rooms on the Club floor and keeping them clean. The janitress shall have charge of the halls and rooms of members in the third and fourth stories and the keeping of them clean and such other duties as the Assistant Secretary may require, and shall be under the control of the Assistant Secretary, subject to the House Committee.

RULE 15.

There shall be no charge for the use of the billiard or pool tables. No person shall use the tables more than one hour if they are wanted by others. Any damage done to the tables, balls or cues, must be paid for by the person causing the same.

RULE 16.

No gaming shall be permitted in the Club rooms.

RULE 17.

Ladies accompanied by members may visit the Club building on Thursday between the hours of 10 o'clock, A. M., to 12 o'clock, P. M., and at such other times and under such regulations as the House Committee may prescribe.

RULE 18.

The names of the House Committee shall be posted in the Club house.

Members of Dallas Club
January 1st, 1899

Resident Members

1887	Abrams, W. H.	1898	Clark, T. I.
1896	Adams, H. W.	1893	Clark, W. H.
1890	Adoue, J. B.	1888	Cobb, C. C.
1887	Aldridge, A. D.	1887	Cochran, S. P.
1898	Allen, A. A.	1897	Connor, W. O.
1898	Allen, J. W.	1898	Cooke, Hamilton
1897	Allen, R. B.	1888	Craddock, L.
1888	Avery, J. M.	1898	Craig, Norman
		1898	Cravens, J. R.
1887	Back, Walter	1887	Crawford, M. L.
1898	Barry, Chas. S.	1895	Craycroft, H. A.
1887	Belo, A. H.	1896	Crush, W. G.
1899	Belo, A. H., Jr.	1898	Curlin, J. L.
1890	Bessard, A.	1899	Childress, W. A.
1896	Bickham, W. L.	1899	Collier, T. N.
1894	Bonner, W. A.		
1898	Brown, A. J.		
1887	Burt, H. F.	1893	Dabney, L. M.
		1898	Dargan, L.
		1898	Dargan, V. C.
1894	Cabell, B. E.	1888	Dexter, C. L.
1899	Cairnes, R. C.	1889	Doremus, F.
1899	Callier, E. R.	1894	Duke, J. C.
1892	Camp, T. L.		
1898	Carlton, O. S.		
1888	Carnes, J. J.	1898	Eberly, E. S.
1896	Cary, A. P.	1892	Edwards, H. L.
1898	Cary, J. M.	1896	Edwards, E. S.
1898	Childress, A. W.	1898	Ellis, E. A.
1898	Claiborne, H.	1892	Everman, J. W.
1898	Claiborne, P. G.	1888	Ewing, A. L.

1898	Fairbanks, H. W.	1892	Hughes, L. H.
1898	Feickert, A.	1887	Hughes, J. V.
1887	Ferris, R. A.	1892	Hunter, J. G.
1895	Fife, J. G.		
1898	Flippen, E. L.	1898	Jackson, A. A.
1895	Florian, P. A.	1897	Jackson, A. S.
1897	Foster, G. W.	1898	Jarreau, M. G.
1897	Fowlkes, Jack	1892	Jones, Lawrence
1892	Freeman, T. J.		
1891	Freeman, W. M.	1898	Kahler, H. A.
		1892	Kaufman, M. L.
1895	Galbreath, W. V.	1887	Keating, C. A.
1892	Gannon, E. J.	1890	Keating, H. S.
1891	Gaston, R. K.	1891	Kingsley, T. H.
1897	Gaston, W. H., Jr.	1898	Kinney, C. C.
1896	Gearhart, A. S.		
1899	Ginn, P. E.	1898	Langdeau, C. H.
1887	Gray, Edward	1898	Lauve, T. L.
1895	Green, Geo. H.	1894	Leake, Sam A.
1898	Grice, Wm.	1898	Lee, Geo. H.
1898	Griffin, W. C.	1897	Lehman, Z. M.
1889	Griffiths, T. W.		
1895	Grove, D. E.	1890	Manning, T. A.
1898	Gulick, J. A.	1893	Manning, W. W.
		1898	Marshal, Eugene
1887	Hall, W. L.	1892	Matthews, F. D.
1898	Hamilton, E. T.	1896	Maxwell, J. W.
1887	Hamilton, Henry	1890	Middleton, J. C.
1898	Harral, Whitfield	1887	Miller, Seth
1888	Harry, D. W. C.	1898	Miller, Thos. D.
1898	Hatch, Harry J.	1887	Miller, T. S.
1894	Hill, Bennett	1898	Milliken, S. E.
1887	Holland, F. P.	1898	Mitchell, R. H.
1898	Howard, J. T.	1892	Monagan, T. L.

1898	Morgan, S. T.	1898	Seay, Dero
1888	Moroney, W. J.	1898	Seay, H. L.
1891	Murphy, J. T.	1898	Shannon, M. B.
1837	McCormick, J. M.	1898	Shelmire, J. B.
1890	McElhone, F. H.	1893	Shields, K.
1897	McEntire, W. R.	1898	Shumard, M. A.
1897	McGahey, H. H.	1887	Simpson, J. N.
1894	McReynolds, J. O.	1897	Slaughter, E. D.
		1898	Smallwood, T. R.
1898	Noel, Thomas	1898	Smith, H. B.
1887	Nott, Cooper	1899	Smith, R. N. G.
		1895	Snyder, Oliver
		1897	Stewart, R. H.
1887	O'Connor, J. C.	1898	Stratton, S. T., Jr.
1895	Oeland, I. R.	1898	Stratton, W. H., Jr.
		1887	Stuart, A. H.
1887	Philp, S.	1892	Stuart, E. A.
1887	Pires, L. A.	1887	Sumpter, Guy
1894	Pittman, G. H.	1895	Sweeney, Edgar
1895	Plowman, G. H.	1893	Swope, J.
1887	Potter, R. E.		
1898	Prather, Ed	1889	Taber, A. B.
		1898	Terrell, Roy
1887	Reardon, E. M.	1898	Terrell, S. L.
1899	Reeves, E. J.	1898	Terry, H. S.
1898	Reeves, Frank	1887	Thatcher, J. S.
1896	Robertson, A. F.	1887	Thomas, J. D.
		1893	Thompson, Wm.
1895	Sabin, L. S.	1890	Thorne, L. S.
1887	Sanger, A.	1898	Tighe, E. M.
1887	Sanger, P.	1898	Tomlin, A. V.
1892	Sargent, E. L.	1887	Townsend, W. J.
1895	Scarff, W. G.	1887	Trezevant, J. T.
1887	Schneider, J. E.	1887	Tucker, C. F.

1898	Tucker, S. G. B.	1898	Wendelken, F. S.
1887	Turner, E. P.	1892	Wernse, A. H.
		1887	Wilkins, A. H.
1897	Vardell, T. W.	1897	Wilson, J. B.
1897	Walker, G. F.	1887	Wood, J. L.
1898	Waters, W. M.		
1888	Wathen, B. S.	1898	Yopp, W. I.

Non-Resident Members

1893	Adams, H. H. . . . . Hearne, Texas
1895	Aiken, C. H. . . . . Texarkana, Texas
1890	Carrow, Richard . . . . . . Henrietta, Texas
1898	Cate, H. M. . . . . Mineola, Texas
1891	Cronkhite, J. A. . . . . Dallas, Texas
1888	Culberson, C. A. . . . . Dallas, Texas
1888	Dunlap, O. E. . . . . . Waxahachie, Texas
1898	Evans, A. W. W. . . . . Dallas, Texas
1898	George, R. E. . . . . Houston, Texas
1898	Goodwin, Osce . . . . . Waxahachie, Texas
1893	Green, E. H. R. . . . . Terrell, Texas
1889	Grinnan, J. S. . . . . Terrell, Texas
1887	Hickox, M. H. . . . . Dallas, Texas
1888	Huey, J. . . . . Corsicana, Texas
——	Jones, J. H. . . . . Houston, Texas
1897	Lewis, J. C. . . . . Austin, Texas
1890	Lovett, R. S. . . . . Houston, Texas
1898	Lowe, R. G. . . . . Galveston, Texas
1896	Lyon, Cecil A. . . . . Sherman, Texas
1898	Mitchell, J. E. . . . . Fort Worth, Texas
1898	Munn, T. J. . . . . Austin, Texas

1898	McKenzie, J. F.	San Angelo, Texas
1898	McQueen, R. C.	Waco, Texas
1897	Nash, W. T.	Kaufman, Texas
1887	O'Connor, J. F.	Galveston, Texas
1897	Payne, Jno. B.	Fort Worth, Texas
1898	Pescay, C. H.	Houston, Texas
1899	Phillips, John O.	Austin, Texas
1898	Polk, L. J.	Galveston, Texas
1887	Quinlan, G. A.	Houston, Texas
1892	Robertson, F. D.	Dallas, Texas
1894	Robinson, Thos. A.	Galveston, Texas
1898	Simpson, W. Sloan	Dallas, Texas
1897	Slattery, J. M.	Dallas, Texas
1898	Stratton, Hugh	Dallas, Texas
1895	Summerfield, Jno.	Dallas, Texas
1892	Tufts, J. P.	Dallas, Texas
1897	Turner, Geo. H.	Palestine, Texas
1897	Warner, S. G.	Tyler, Texas
1892	Warren, J. C.	Dallas, Texas
1897	Warren, J. T.	Dallas, Texas
1897	Wolfenden, C. F.	Dallas, Texas

Honorary Members

Enders, Wm.	St. Louis, Missouri
Grant, Capt. Jno. A.	Atlanta, Georgia
Henry, Judge Jno. L.	Dallas, Texas
Shepard, Hon. Seth	Washington, D. C.
Toland, Geo. W.	Denver, Colorado

In Memoriam

JAMES AIKEN, ... March 23, 1896

B. C. ADOUE. . . . . . . July 28, 1892

W. L. ARMSTRONG, ... June 14, 1891

MARC BESSARD, . . . February 5, 1896

JOHN C. BROWN, ... August 17, 1889

J. W. BUSTER, ... April 6, 1898

J. A. CARROLL, ... October 12, 1891

JAMES H. DILLARD, . . . March 15, 1892

A. S. DOUGLAS, ... June 3, 1893

W. H. FLIPPEN, ... January 17, 1891

JOHN T. GANO, . . . November 2, 1891

JOHN HARES, ... March 9, 1896

L. M. KNEPFLY, . . September 18, 1898

LOUIS E. MOHRHARDT, . . Nov. 8, 1888

JAMES R. MERRYFIELD, . . Sept. 7, 1889

B. W. McCULLOUGH, . January 21, 1892

E. H. ROBERTSON, ... June 22, 1890

SAWNIE ROBERTSON, . . . June 27, 1892

L. S. ROSS, ... January 3, 1898

W. H. RYAN, ... October 14, 1888

A. D. H. SILVER, ... June 13, 1895

A. W. STEWART, . . September 17, 1897

J. W. WEBB, ... September 19, 1891